Balboa Press books may be ordered through booksellers or by contacting:

Balboa Press
A Division of Hay House
1663 Liberty Drive
Bloomington, IN 47403
www.balboapress.com
844-682-1282

ISBN: 978-1-9822-7526-6 (sc)
978-1-9822-7527-3 (e)

Library of Congress Control Number: 2021919992

Print information available on the last page.

Balboa Press rev. date: 10/28/2021

BALBOA.PRESS
A DIVISION OF HAY HOUSE

Born to be Treasured

Preethi, a Jewel in His Hand

Adventure 1

Look into those eyes.

That is you.

We know diamonds are of great and special value; so are you.

So is Preethi. Her name means "love."

Spring

Preethi is thinking.

Some bizarre virus with its ugly, dangerous crown and long spikes came to bring chaos; the whole world froze. In fact, the whole world stopped to breathe, just like the virus caused people to stop breathing. What a hostage. It's unfair.

It's all about technology: "I'm all time at home with my family, missing my friends."

Will school still be coming? Do I matter? What can I do? I am bored. Will I see my friends? Will I catch the virus at school? What really happened? What is behind all of it? Frankly, I don't care; I just want to live. I want my family and friends alive.

What is freedom now? We don't know. It's a cloud of mystery.

The TV screen on the main street nearby shows awful images. Preethi observes that it is not only the coronavirus; what about other diseases, isolation, rejection, violence, pollution, poverty, slavery, control, depression, and so on? Yes, what about technology—can it save us?

In this virus freeze time, we had fun too, she thinks. Neighbors and their kids were dancing on their balcony, clapping hands, at eight o'clock in the evening, encouraging the medical team to find a solution to stop the virus. We all loved that part.

Such a weird time. And in the midst of all this, Preethi is alive.

What keeps her alive and will continue to keep her? Come and dive in the wise gems and special keys that Preethi will encounter on her journey in NowLand.

In Her Golden Boots

She is loved in a normal way, she thinks.

Preethi is a thirteen-year-old with vivid blue-green eyes and frizzy hair. Her skin has a special color. One arm is transparent, like liquid; it is beautiful. She is fluid and beautiful. Nevertheless, she's not considered pretty by her surroundings. She is different, and honestly, she doesn't know where she belongs. It affects her confidence in herself. She wipes away those thoughts by looking and dressing older than she is. Quite often, she does grown-up stuff. In this world, can she still be a sneaky daddy's girl?

In the city where she lives, there are not many girls. Her homeland is a superpower with different nations and an amazing amount of diversity. The leaders are concerned about the environment and the continual betterment of the school system. Every year she sees a lot of tourists.

Deep down, she has the qualities of a true queen and the heart of a lion. But that heart is often like coal, darkened by pain. She often lies to survive, like everybody. But in that way, she is not true to herself, especially when she feels misunderstood. She is misunderstood and rejected in the neighborhood and sometimes at school. There are many noises and voices around her.

She likes to binge-watch media to gain information. And yet now and then, it is too much. "Hello," Preethi says. "Do they not notice?"

She lives with her mom and two brothers. Her mom is a data detective. Her dad is not often around. She hopes he is a space pilot. She thinks her family is normal. What is normal? They have all their separate TV memberships. Is there enough time for true care or personal care? Her two brothers are fun and, of course, also annoying.

Her family loves her in their way. Her lack of confidence makes tears often drop on her cheek and into the well of her lips. Her voice is silenced when she feels intimidated. What more is hidden in her heart?

Pause.

It's a velvet soft-blue sky day. After all those months locked up because of the virus, she is happy to see her few friends and to smell the school walls again. She even missed teacher Mad-o. During this freeze time, the school, normally well equipped, has still a deserted atmosphere. Preethi likes school. When she was little, Preethi loved her preschool classes there.

"It is good to see friends and school again." She shrugs with relief.

Suddenly, some droplets of dust trickle beside her from up in the classroom ceiling. "What is this—another virus, another invasion?"

As she looks closer, she sees strangers, miniature robots, androids, and drones.

She can't believe her eyes! With her mouth open, she nudges her friend with an elbow. But all her classmates and her teacher have fallen asleep. Now she is alone and isolated again.

In a split second, Preethi is taken away. Her head tolls; flashing thoughts rush through her mind: *I'm sorry and worried. I miss my mom and my dad too. And my annoying brothers. I am so sorry for my lies, my "I know" and "yes but." Is there still hope for me to see my friends and family again?*

It seems as if Preethi is going to learn what life is about. The lively blue-green eyes of the liquid-armed one show a mix of despair and anguish. She freezes and lands in survival mode. Her autodestruction button is easily pushed. "Who can help me now and meet all my needs?"

For these specific droplets, not all that glitters is gold.

In the dusty place where she is, a spectacular clash of dark and light is going on. She is snatched out of the hands of dark.

She pauses and looks at the spectacular Awesome Light of God. It is just in front of her.

Neither her eyes nor her heart have never seen such a light.

The Awesome Light of God smiles at her.

She feels a light and awesome love, one that she has really never known before.

The Awesome Light of God says, "I knew you before you were in your mother's womb."

In a nanosecond, she steps in her golden boots of confidence in God. One more step, and she is in the hand of the Awesome Light of God. She chooses to trust and not fear and to give the new situation a try.

She is lifted higher, up into the sky.

NowLand

From the hand of the Awesome Light of God, she takes some more steps up. A door stands open. And as she comes closer to the door, a voice says, "I am Jasper."

He pops up; he is crystal clear, like water.

How odd! She is startled. Why is he crystal clear? Sometimes his color changes red. Then she realizes that her arm has this transparent liquid color too. She feels accepted and challenges herself to open up. The girl realizes that she is already in an extraspecial situation. Even though it is not easy for her to trust, she tries.

Preethi says, "My name is—"

Bzzbzzzz—a bot on a squat is noisy and annoying her. *Bzzzzzzzzzz. Bzzzzzzz.*

The boy or thing—what is he, as a matter of fact?

He says, "I can't hear you. What are you saying?"

With a louder voice, Preethi answers, "My name means 'love.'"

"That is interesting," he replies.

On Jasper's forehead, she sees the letters FUTURE passing by. Another word is appearing too: TRANSFORMATION. After each word, the same sentence is repeated: "Let your eyes look straight ahead; fix your gaze directly before you."

"What does it mean?" she asks him.

He responds: "You have favor today, girl. Because you meet with me, you will discover some qualities that will be reflected in you. I bring great turnaround and big-time goodwill. There is a good chance you will adopt splendid beauty and royalty. I bring a bright, new change in your situation."

Preethi answers, "Why do I need to be adopted? I have a family. What do you mean, adoption?"

She goes crazy. There must be something about the adoption.

Bzzz, bzzz—a lot of noise still surrounds them.

She dodges what her new friend is telling her.

"Leave me alone," Preethi screams. "I like tech and gadgets. I program and build cool ones."

Bzzzz, bzzz.

"Why is this one so noisy and annoying?" There is silence in her head.

She continues: "I have noticed something, Jasper. With my classmates and friends, we always have competitions on our gadgets. I was hard on myself and demanding of my classmates. When I was saying something like, 'Oh, you don't have a smoby,' I looked low. Or I just went for long hours and days without my family, locked up with my robots. It didn't bother them, my mum and dad; both my parents were working like crazy. Is there enough time for us?"

Full of love, Jasper nods and says, "Because those tech toys needed all your time and attention. They are machines, but they want what we all want in life—that special kind of love. That indescribable attention. Do you want to know what love is, Preethi?"

Jasper pauses for a bit and then continues. "The greatest gift I ever received was a big apology when I missed it all. Dealing in tech traffic as an addiction, just to be cool, I completely missed it all. I am fifteen now," Jasper says, smiling with relief. "I am telling you: it's best to have friends and family with a pure heart. You tech queen, you will be able to show these robots how to be pure and act with love."

"What are you saying? I don't understand," the girl says.

"The question is, who are you really, Preethi? You have to run your race, run your squat."

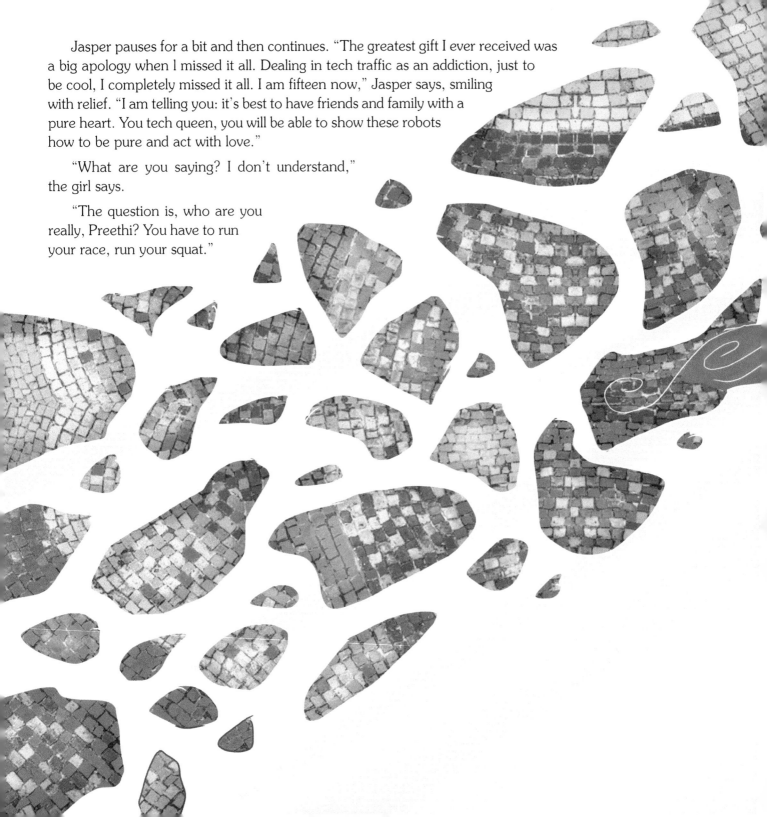

The Awesome Light of God smiles at her.

"Perhaps you don't know me. I was there long before the coronavirus. I am older than your dad and your mum and your brothers. I am more than one thousand generations before and more than one thousand generations to come.

"You are my intention, Preethi; before I formed you in the womb of your mum, I knew you. The very hairs of your head are all numbered. If you know the differences between light and dark in you and around you, let go of the dark, and I, God, will lead you into a greater light."

I am telling you, have friends and family with a pure heart.

As Preethi hears this, her heart swells with more light. Right away, her body and mind start growing. How odd!

Her golden boots of confidence are dancing, and so are Jasper's crystal-clear feet. They are having fun. They are transported through the solar system to another land. NowLand is fun!

Fear Cloud Away

What is happening now?

In NowLand, they are dancing, rejoicing, and dancing some more.

Dark cloud robots are still buzzing around them, still being annoying!

"What? The robots are becoming huge! But why?" Fear overcomes Preethi.

"We must go!" says Jasper.

Goodness, Preethi and Jasper are swelling, like bread made with yeast.

They are uplifted.

"Come; let's step higher in this glass elevator that so we move up in time. There, perhaps, we won't be disturbed by the dark squat," she hastily instructs.

Looking at the fingerprints and codes on the inside of the elevator, Preethi tries to understand Sapphi, who has joined them. "Is this me? Is this who I am?" she asks.

"Yep! If you forget past worries, pains, shame, and 'yes buts,' you will travel in this elevator and will discover your true DNA, all your talents, and the progress you can make."

Preethi looks at Sapphi with big *eyes. I have been scanned*, she realizes. *They know more about me than I do. I should know more about myself.* Preethi speeds up her thoughts and says, "I want to know more!"

She observes Sapphi.

"How cool! Sapphi is so immense intense and kind."

He continues explaining to Preethi: "You will travel through and find all your likes, dislikes, gifts, and possibilities. You'll learn more about your identity and what you are born for. Never forget your true blueprint, and you'll become it, no doubt! You'll be the favored child of the Awesome Light of God. Do not believe the lie that you do not matter. Unlearn this by getting rid of the lies. And know tears of joy bring great relief. You are very precious to your family, us, your neighbors, classmates, people, and the Awesome Light of God."

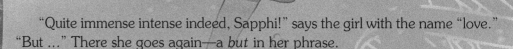

"Quite immense intense indeed, Sapphi!" says the girl with the name "love." "But …" There she goes again—a *but* in her phrase.

"But," she asks, "why do I lie so often to myself, and to others? Why do my surroundings lie? In fact, why is the whole world lying?"

Preethi contemplates; she truly wants to discover that blueprint and the truth.

Sapphi's eyes glow once more, his blue becoming even brighter. Its stones are the source of sapphires, and it contains gold dust. Under Preethi's feet, there is a paved work of sapphire stone, and it is like the heavens in its clarity.

Spectacular!

He tells her, "If you want, you can make me your home, if you are grounded and rooted in my light and love."

Never forget your true design!

Preethi's mind opens as she sees the possibilities. *Wow, surely if I follow my design, with the help of the Awesome Light of God and my new friends, Jasper and Sapphi, I will get a glimpse at the great reward. And I can probably live it. And my family and friends can live it too.*

Let's try.

The elevator lurches; they are going up.

The Friend "Chip"

There is no end to the glass elevator, but they step out of it. It is the right place to do so. They greet Chalce. Preethi ponders and grimaces: "Oh! What is this new one bringing?" Actually, she gets caught herself and must agree, looking at Chalce.

Chalce looks like a joyful song; her moves are a warm, sweet sea breeze. Our liquid-armed girl must sneakily admit that she actually needs such a breeze.

This wave of overwhelming joy is remarkable. The wave brings them into unstoppable laughter and tears and laughter again. They give their all, with no calculation, just releasing their emotions—both Preethi and her friends. Their bellies are shaking and hurting from the laughter and jokes they are sharing. They are singing *thank you* to everything they are thankful for.

In Preethi's pondering, she wonders how *thank you* would smell, something the tech queen has never thought about before. She knows how it would sound and look. Chalce is indeed quite something!

Chalce catches Preethi's thoughts and responds: "You know my key? As I joyfully laugh to life and am thankful for all things little and big, I believe more in myself, my gifts, and my talents. With this thinking, all dark clouds, insecurity, and discomfort just run away. No fear, no doubt, no failure—the Awesome Light of God is with me."

Before Chalce leaves, she downloads all her gifts from her hands to Preethi's hands.

Be a sweet smelling perfume breeze!

The Awesome Light of God smiles at her.

The Awesome Light of God nods. "Embrace the gifts Chalce handed over to you. I created you in my image. It gives me great joy to see you grow in those precious gifts. That is wisdom."

Preethi, full of grateful laughter, opens her hand. She sees the power and peace of the Awesome Light of God flowing through her. This token of friendship is like a fresh morning.

There is no complaining, and life is fair all the time. Right now, Preethi's hands are glowing with a blue-green light, the color of her eyes.

Chalce, Sapphi, and Preethi can't stop laughing. She feels like a hero with attitude; she doesn't know all the answers and still just took a giant step of trust.

"Who is laughing so hard?" says a voice.

"Ah, Emer, join us! Wow, Emer, you look stunning. Where have you been? You must have been at a laser game."

Emer replies, "Well, it was like this." He projects a glimpse of White Wood.

An image appears of a forest full of trees, white palm trees flourishing and cedars of Lebanon growing everywhere.

"Beautiful, though the color of that wood is weird!" says the one with the blue-green eyes. In the midst of the flourishing palms and cedars, she sees people-trees.

These people-trees are men, women, kids, aunties, uncles, nieces, nephews, and grandparents—all kinds of people.

They are indeed like trees. It moves Preethi.

Emer turns off the laser projector in his hand.

"You see, I was not alone," he explains. "I needed help, and the kids in the wood needed me too. We were five thousand, so I had to stay courageous and truly be there for those in need. It is good to stand up for justice and freedom. These people-trees were once seeds of justice and freedom, the smallest of all seeds. Yet when they grow, they are the largest of garden plants and become trees, and the birds come and perch in their branches."

Emer pauses.

"Can you imagine the justice and freedom? Do you know what justice and freedom are?" he asks Preethi, Jasper, and Chalce.

He continues. "They are working as a team, each with his or her touch, helping one another for the greater good. And then the mighty hand of the Awesome Light of God brings ease, peace, and speed, making everything just awesome."

Preethi looks at him with big eyes, at first furious and then sad.

Right now, her growing confidence cracks and is weakening.

Emer comforts her, saying, "Let us draw near to the Awesome Light of God with a genuine heart and with the full assurance that faith brings. He surrounds His people both now and forevermore."

Preethi doesn't know what to say.

Slowly she whispers, "What can I do, Emer?"

He replies, "You can do all things through the Awesome Light of God, who gives you strength. We can stand in His place if we keep our hearts and hands pure."

He says to Preethi, "Yes, I want to do good to people with all my fortune; I want to rejoice over them as I do over you. I rejoice over you to do you good, with all My heart and with all My soul, and I will continue to do it. If you seek me with all your heart and all your soul, you will find me. Call me, and I will answer you and show you great and mighty things that you do not know."

Preethi cannot ignore it longer. "This is so special; I feel small and big at the same time. It would be nice to not do my own little story but to love as you love, Awesome Light of God. That love is something!"

Our leading lady is longing for more. Her heart cries, "Teach me more! Teach me how to find my place in your team, to help and to be helped. Thank you for letting me shine through your truth and splendor like never before."

She burst out, flowing like a fountain.

The Awesome Light of God smiles at her.

She remembers Emer's glowing hand, a projector. She recalls the picture of the fascinating wood and its people-trees. When she does so, the word lula pops into her mind. This is it—she knows how deepdown knowing feels. She just knows this is it: lula! The word echoes in her mind.

Indeed, the voice in her is speaking: "Let us not become weary in doing good. You can do it—create lula! You are not alone; you will find more friends like Jasper, Sapphi, Chalce, and Emer. You will find the right truth and do right.":

White Wood Autumn

The courageous Preethi moves into autumn with her team.

Our girl is looking at her new friends; she appreciates her team with a loving wink.

She is musing and wondering, "What can I do to make life better for the people-trees living in White Wood?"

She hears the Awesome Light of God very well, saying: "Love and faithfulness meet; goodness (uprightness) and peace kiss each other. Faithfulness springs forth from the earth, and goodness (uprightness) looks down from heaven. You and all your new friends will stand and see the big reward—your wonderful place."

Which reward? Which wonderful place? "That sounds good," she says, chuckling.

The Awesome Light of God smiles at her.

Preethi's eyes smile back.

He tells her, "Eyes have not seen, and ears have not heard, nor have the things the Awesome Light of God prepared for those who love Him entered into the heart of humanity."

Preethi breathes and whispers, "Awesome Light of God, I love to be your princess. Jesus, I ask you to be always in my heart."

It is done, precious one! The Awesome Light of God Himself loves her. He says, "Because you have loved Me and have believed that I came from the Awesome Light of God."

A great rest comes over our little hero. Her heart completes her thought: "Peaceful home in me—that is the Awesome Light of God. Thank you for calling me onward and upward. Your will be done; let your kingdom come into my heart and my life this day. I trust what is coming. I am born to be treasured. I am a jewel in His hand. And so will be the people-trees of White Wood. *Lula* and my friends will help me."

ERROR CODE:01001

ERROR CODE:01001

ERROR COD

ERRO

ERROR COD

The end. A new beginning.

Yes, He who sits on the throne said, "Behold, I am making all things new."

Discover how Preethi, her friends, and *lula* experience a new beginning.

BIG thank you to My Father, who loves me so majestically. Writing a book and living this life, it is special and more rewarding than I could imagine. Impossible without your great help. You helped me unlock so many doors. Your believe in me, your nature, patience and your calmness are memorable.

Precious reader, bright gem, may YOU have a skyward perspective of life after reading the book. Go and shine forever!

To the kids of de Vrije basisschool Terbank-Egenhoven Belgium 2018: thank you for letting me spent time with you! Pauline, you were, at that precise moment, such a meaningful mirror to me.

Maman Christine, thank you for my nickname « 1kg de diamant ». My warmest gratitude for your unconditional love.

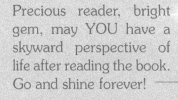

Mummy & daddy, Dr. Richard & Pr. Catherine Onebamoi, you are priceless resources who enriched me far beyond I could ever think! The quality of your love, profoundness, sagacity and constant support despite life struggles met, helped me to restore my DNA.

Jan & Iris Gillisjan, two amazing persons in my life, your remarkable love, joy helped me to reach freedom and major progress in my life. Thank you for your friendship, advice and wisdom-filled talks.

Nathan, Naomi-Lisha, Nethania and Nearia -Destinie Onebamoi, I enjoyed so much your genuine care, brilliance and simplicity, it just ignited my mind vividly.

Dr. Francis & Pr. Carmela Myles, what a peculiar love and acumen you reflect! You led me to a deeper understanding of life and technologies; Your work and brilliance continue to floor me.

The one who taught me to read, write and flickered the light for books in my heart, I say thank you schoolteacher Simonne, my godmother. Simonne & Walter Adriaenssens-Claes many thanks for your ever support.

Big heart Caroline, the home you reserved for me during the book process was an opportunity for inspiration, I really appreciate it.

Thank you LLK, the challenges with you helped me to crystalize my potential

To my mentors, your lumimous mentorship helped me to kickstart the journey and give me the audacity to publically unveil this book.

Grateful for one of my greatest gifts, inspiration and appreciation, my awesome husband.

Toua Travaglini, I experienced your delicate care and the continuing faith in the birthing process of this book and in my life as momentous. You were just like an angel. Paolo Travaligni, thank you so much for your respect and grateful heart.

To my magnificent babies, you are precious treasures. The part of me will always be in your gratitude for thrilling me with this book.

Praise, Lambert, Sam, Asy, Isy, Jean-Max, Sandra & Sam Mayaka, all noteworthy gems who shaped the diamond in me; I learned so much, thanks, merci beaucoup!

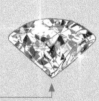

Fabienne Malfait, your love and presence on the journey was like a warm sunshine to me, indispensable.

Bénédicte Onebamoi and Psalmiste Kristy, great thanks for your crucial significant contributions in my life.

Balboa Press, your professional publishing capacity stretched me beyond my dreams and led to an amazing job done. Angel Fremont, Hera Bennett, James Yano and the exquisite Illustration Team who helped turn a raw draft into something meaningful, you guys are unforgettable.

EditorBrightMc, the spark of every word came to life by your editing, what a significant help.

Donna Partow, your "God-confidence", beauty and humor are an inestimable boost to my life and the book. Mary Trask thank you for your book, a notable support in my researches.

Jean Luc Rowerga, the remarkable storyteller in you and your life helped me to aspire to develop more nobility in my character.

Titi & Frank Dewitte-Mullie, your lifework, your way of building up people, inspired me and the book.

Olivia Binana, Litsa Fidanidis, Carine & Annaelle Kwayep and Pascale Janssens, I will remember your encouragement at crucial moments, they gave me confidence to move forward.

You are a treasure!

From Me to You

Precious one—yes, you—
You are invaluable, and your splendor is infinite.
Yours, Guébli Carron

Bringing stars and galaxies down

to earth as a new chance

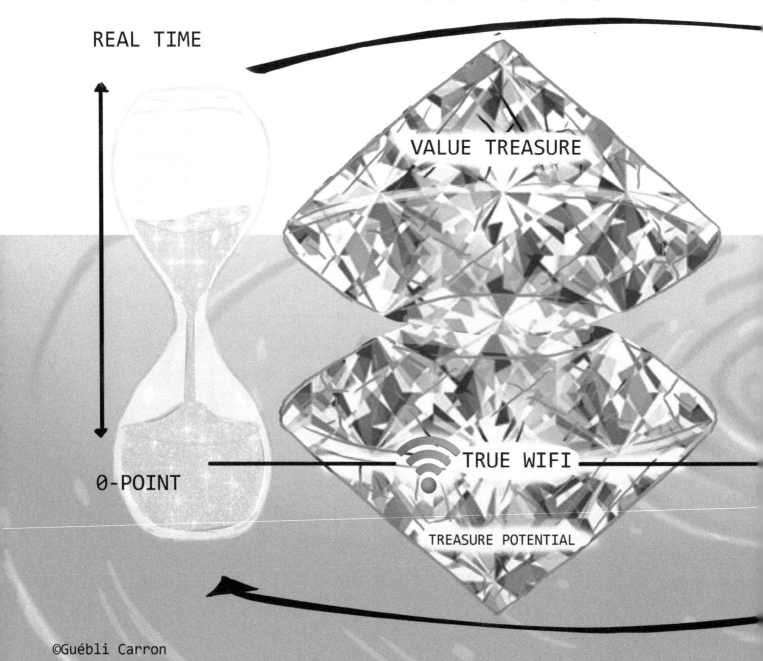

"REAL-DEAL" MODEL
MICRO-MACRO NEEDS

REAL TIME

VALUE TREASURE

0-POINT

TRUE WIFI

TREASURE POTENTIAL

©Guébli Carron

KINGDOM CULTURE

3. TRUTH - MIND

2. TRUTH - DNA INVESTMENT

LIGHT IMPACT

1. TRUTH - LOVE

Johan Van Droogenbroeck, image- zone.be ©2020.

*Ingrid Van Droogenbroeck***, you made a milestone difference
in my life and in many other lives.**